Goldilocks And The Three Bears

Once upon a time, in a far-off country, there lived a little girl named Goldilocks. She lived in a pretty little cottage at the edge of the forest. Her mother had warned her not to go out into the woods alone, and Goldilocks, like a good girl, obeyed her mother.

Goldilocks did not have any brothers or sisters or friends, so she was quite lonely. She played by herself all day long.

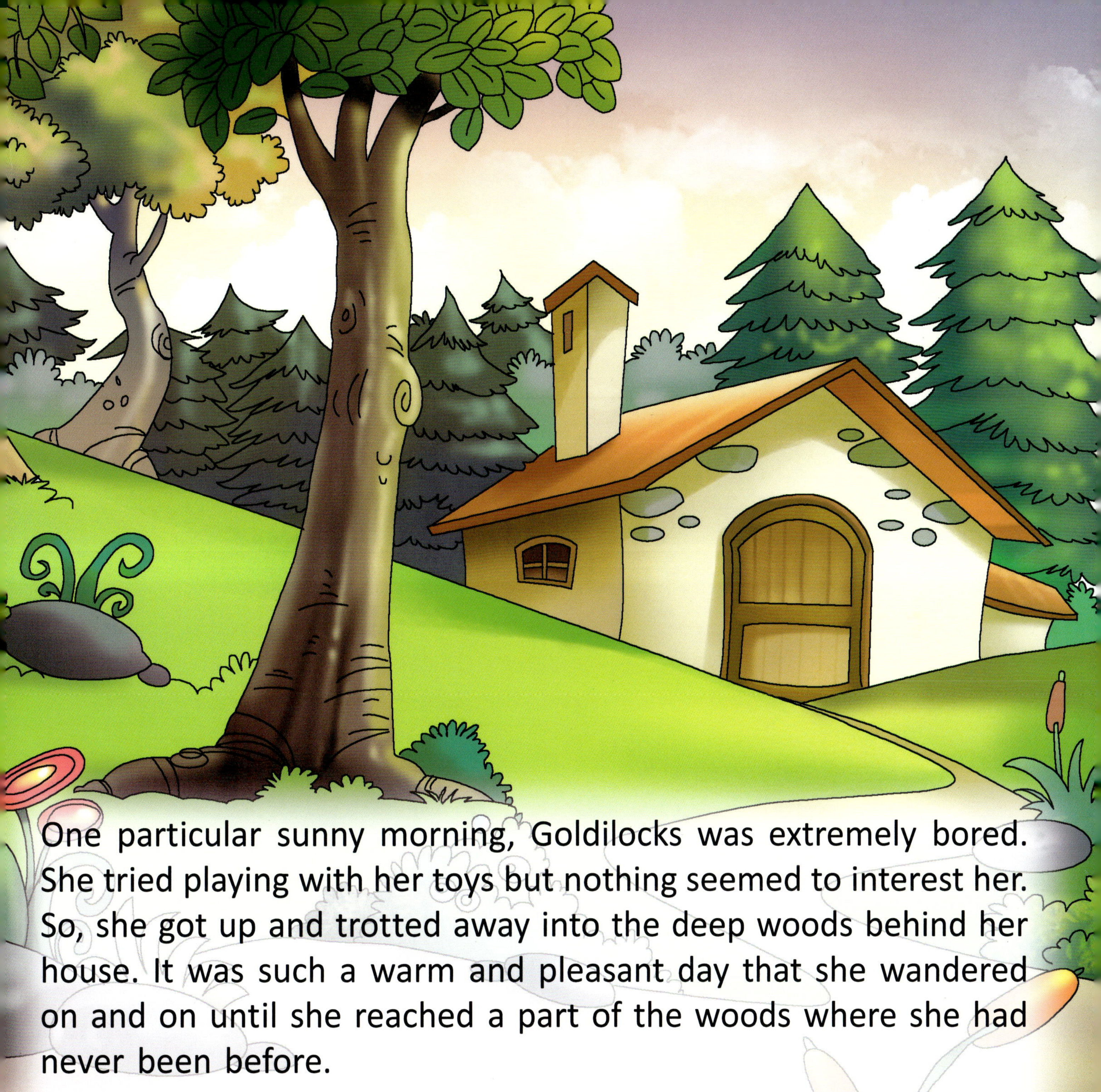

One particular sunny morning, Goldilocks was extremely bored. She tried playing with her toys but nothing seemed to interest her. So, she got up and trotted away into the deep woods behind her house. It was such a warm and pleasant day that she wandered on and on until she reached a part of the woods where she had never been before.

In this part of the woods, lived a family of three bears. The first was a great big bear, the Father Bear; the second was a middle-sized bear, the Mother Bear; and the third was a teeny-weeny bear, their one and only baby. They all lived together in a funny little house, and were very happy there. Goldilocks stopped at the door of the house, and wondered who lived there.

"I'll just go in and see," she thought, and entered the house, but no one was there. The bears had all gone out for a morning walk. The porridge they were going to have for their meal was kept on the table.

Goldilocks was rather tired after her walk, and the porridge smelt so good that she began to feel hungry. Although she looked everywhere, she could not find anyone, and at last, she could resist no longer. She decided to take just a little bite of the porridge.

The porridge had been put into three bowls—a great big bowl for Father Bear, a middle-sized bowl for Mother Bear, and a teeny-weeny bowl for Baby Bear. Goldilocks picked up a spoon with her dainty little fingers, and ate a spoonful of porridge from the great big bowl.

"Ugh! It is so hot!" she cried out. Since she was very hungry, she thought she would try from another bowl.

This time, she took a big spoonful of Mother Bear's porridge, but she liked that no better, for it was also very hot. But when she tasted the teeny-weeny Bear's porridge, it was just as she would like her porridge, so she ate up every tiny bit of it.

When Goldilocks had finished her meal, she noticed three chairs by the wall. One was a great big chair. With great difficulty, she climbed and sat on it.

"Oh dear! How hard it is!" she exclaimed.

She was sure that she could not sit there for long, and so, she climbed up on the middle-sized chair.

However, the middle-sized chair was too soft and cushioned for her taste. So now, she sat on the teeny-weeny chair.

"This is perfect," she said. It was so comfortable that she sat on and on, and happily twisted and turned in it, till the bottom gave away and the tiny chair broke into pieces. But, she did not care. She just got up and began to wonder what to do next.

There was a staircase in the middle of the house. Goldilocks decided to go up and see where it led to. So, up she went, and when she reached the top, she saw that there was a bedroom at the end of the corridor. In the middle of the room, stood a great big bed; on one side of it, was a middle-sized bed; and on the other side, was a teeny-weeny bed.

Goldilocks was sleepy, and so, she thought, “I will just lie down for a while and take a nap.”

So first, she jumped onto the great big bed, but it was just as hard as the great big chair had been. So, she jumped off it and tried the middle-sized bed, but it was so soft that she sank right down into the feather cushions and could hardly breathe.

“I will try the teeny-weeny bed,” she said to herself. It was so comfortable that she soon fell fast asleep.

While Goldilocks was sleeping peacefully, the three bears returned from their walk, very hungry and quite ready to eat their porridge.

But oh dear me! How angry Father Bear looked when he saw his spoon had been used and the table was a mess!

"Who tasted my porridge?" he growled in his great big voice.

"And who tasted mine?" growled Mother Bear, in her middle-sized voice.

"And who tasted mine and ate it all up?" cried the hungry baby bear in his teeny-weeny voice. Tears ran down his teeny-weeny face as he looked at the empty bowl of porridge.

Father Bear was quite angry and upset. He decided to sit and think as to who could have been in the house while they were out.

When Father Bear went to sit down on his great big chair, he cried out in his great big voice, "Who sat on my chair?"

And suddenly, Mother Bear cried out in her middle-sized voice, “Who sat on my chair?”

Then, Baby Bear cried out in his teeny-weeny voice, “Who sat on my chair and broke it into pieces?”

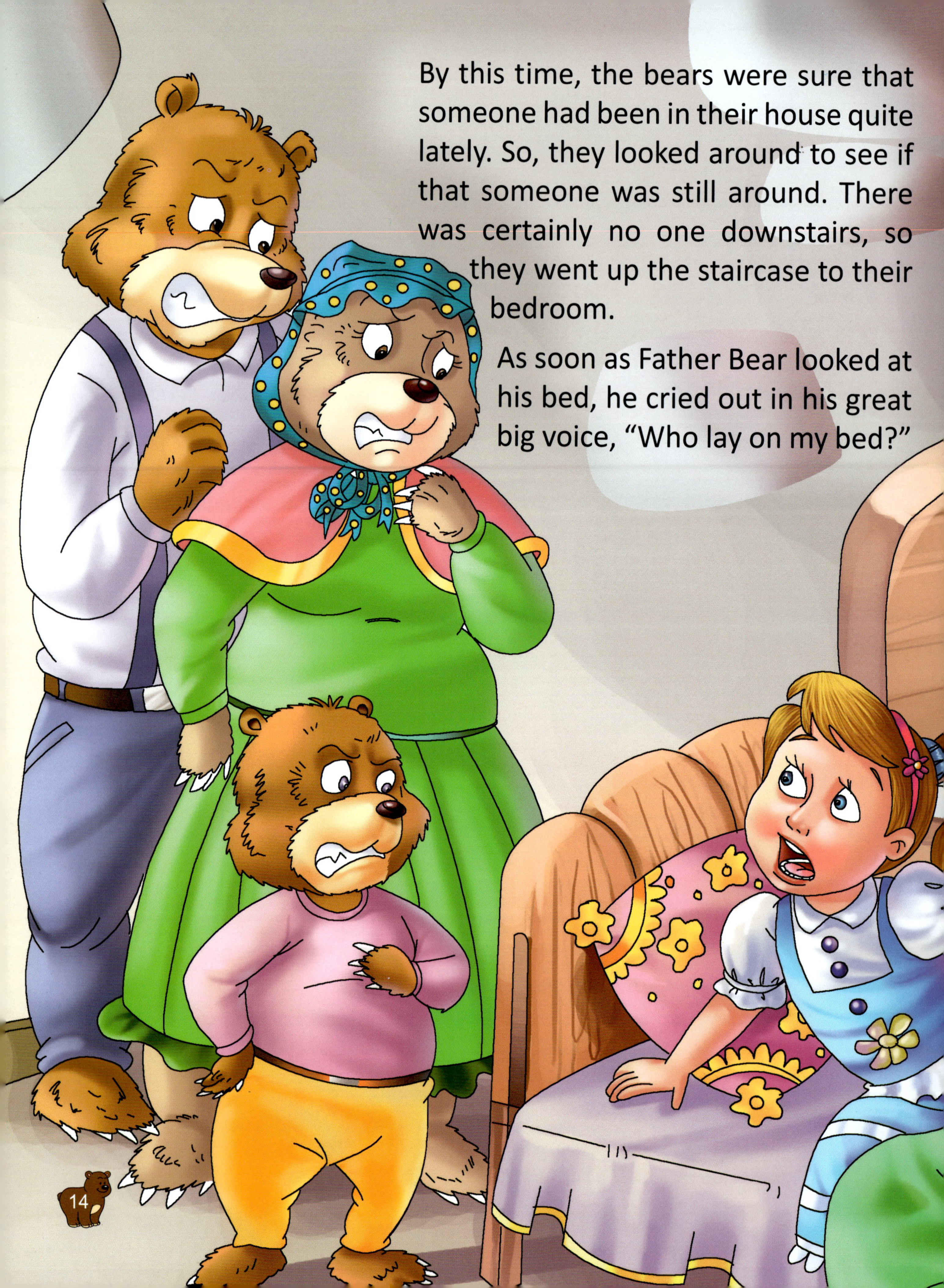

By this time, the bears were sure that someone had been in their house quite lately. So, they looked around to see if that someone was still around. There was certainly no one downstairs, so they went up the staircase to their bedroom.

As soon as Father Bear looked at his bed, he cried out in his great big voice, "Who lay on my bed?"

Mother Bear cried out in her middle-sized voice, “Who lay on my bed?”

Baby Bear cried out in his teeny-weeny voice, “Oh Mother, Father! Look someone is sleeping in my bed!”

Now, when Father Bear started to speak, Goldilocks began dreaming of a little bee buzzing in the room; when Mother Bear began to speak, she dreamt that the bee was flying out of the window; but when Baby Bear began to speak, she felt that the bee had come back and stung her on the ear, and up she jumped. And Oh! How frightened she was when she saw the three bears standing right behind her!

Goldilocks jumped out of the bed and was out of the open window in a trice. Not stopping to even look if she was being followed, she ran and ran until she reached her home. She vowed, then and there, never again to venture into the woods all by herself, and till today, she has indeed kept the promise she made to herself!

Printed in India